# Dear Parent:
## Your child's love of reading starts here!

Every child learns to read in a different way and at his or her own speed. Some go back and forth between reading levels and read favorite books again and again. Others read through each level in order. You can help your young reader improve and become more confident by encouraging his or her own interests and abilities. From books your child reads with you to the first books he or she reads alone, there are I Can Read Books for every stage of reading:

### SHARED READING
Basic language, word repetition, and whimsical illustrations, ideal for sharing with your emergent reader

### BEGINNING READING
Short sentences, familiar words, and simple concepts for children eager to read on their own

### READING WITH HELP
Engaging stories, longer sentences, and language play for developing readers

### READING ALONE
Complex plots, challenging vocabulary, and high-interest topics for the independent reader

I Can Read Books have introduced children to the joy of reading since 1957. Featuring award-winning authors and illustrators and a fabulous cast of beloved characters, I Can Read Books set the standard for beginning readers.

A lifetime of discovery begins with the magical words "I Can Read!"

*Visit www.icanread.com for infoɪ*
*on enriching your child's reading eː*

D0816179

Pinkfong: Everybody Dances!
Copyright © 2023 by The Pinkfong Company, Inc.
All rights reserved. Pinkfong™ is a trademark of The Pinkfong Company, Inc., registered
or pending rights worldwide.
Printed in the United States of America.
No part of this book may be used or reproduced in any manner whatsoever without written permission
except in the case of brief quotations embodied in critical articles and reviews. For information address
HarperCollins Children's Books, a division of HarperCollins Publishers, 195 Broadway, New York, NY 10007.
www.icanread.com

Library of Congress Control Number: 2022944118
ISBN 978-0-06-327245-3

23 24 25 26 27  LB  10 9 8 7 6 5 4 3 2 1     First Edition

# Everybody Dances!

HARPER
*An Imprint of HarperCollinsPublishers*

This is Pinkfong.

Pinkfong is a pink fox.

"Come on,

I want to show you my world!"

Pinkfong says.

This is Nini.
Nini is a cute orange cat
and Pinkfong's best friend.

These friends love
to do everything together.
"Let's go!" Nini says.

This is Mo.

Mo is round and fluffy,

perfect for traveling

on top of Nini's head!

"Wait for me!"
Mo says.

Mo, Nini, and Pinkfong
play together.
They read together.
They even bake together!

But there is one thing
that these friends
love the most.

They love to dance together!

"Time to boogie!" Pinkfong says.

When Pinkfong spins,
Nini twirls.

When Mo jumps,
Pinkfong bumps.

"Can we join in?"
the dancing penguins ask.

"Of course!" Pinkfong says.

It's time to learn the penguin dance.
First, wiggle both flippers.

Then, shake both feet.

Finally, turn around.

That's the penguin dance!

"This is harder
than I thought,"
Nini says.

"There are so many ways
to dance!"
Pinkfong cheers.
"Everybody dances in
their own way."

23

"Let's go find more friends,"
Pinkfong says.
"They will show us
how they dance."

# Great idea!

First stop is to visit Baby Car.
"How do you dance?"
Pinkfong asks.

"I dance like this,"
Baby Car says.
First he beeps,
then he vrooms.

Next stop is to visit Baby T-Rex.

Look!

He brought the whole family.

They make the ground shake
with their dance moves.

Finally, the friends visit
the bus family.

The wheels on the bus
go round and round!

These friends are great dancers.

And so are you!

Keep dancing!